Once Around the Lake

Story by Susan Woods Golder
Pictures by Daniel Traynor

To Miles + Ava
Enjoy the magic
of the outdoors!
Susan Golder

ISBN-13: 978-1511432542 // ISBN-10: 1511432543

Morning Song Press
E. Stoneham, Maine
www.susanwoodsgolder.com

Dedication

To Owen, Charlie, Brody and Josephine: Always capture the magic!

To Courtney, Ashley and Adam for making the camp on the hill such a blessed home.

To Charlie for always keeping the wind in my sails.

Acknowledgments

Sincere thanks to Dan Traynor for his creative inspiration;

to Mary Lois Sanders for her expertise and encouragement;

to the Writers4Kids team for their thoughtful feedback.

Once Around the Lake

Early one morning Odie snoozed in the dark,

with his glasses and pad and his pen being parked

in his lap where he'd left them late last night,

when voices from afar hollered, "Turn out the light!"

See Odie was a boy who, when it was late,

liked to draw and write to remember each date.

He'd lie in his room … he'd wonder and think …

then, by flashlight, he'd write with hardly a blink.

Sometimes, his busy mind bubbled with stuff
till he'd fill up the pages and say, "Enough!"
Then, colorful dreams that were happy and fun
in the calm and the quiet of Odie's night spun.

At the end of the bed lay his puppy dog, Max,
tangled in toys and unable to relax.

At Odie's first stretch, he leaped and he hopped.

This faithful friend, Max, he never forgot.

A dog on a mission knows just what to do.

"Wake up, Odie. It's time to canoe!"

Though Odie might wish he could stay in his bed,

Max brought his leash to be sure he'd be led.

"Time's a wasting!" the wags in his tail suggested.

"Tonight, not today, is your turn to be resting."

With a yawn and a stretch and a nod that was slow,

Odie tossed and he turned, then got ready to go.

"I can count on my Max," he jotted in a fog,

"to make sure I don't live like a bump on a log."

With a fist full of berries and a big bone to throw,

Odie dashed to the dock with Max in tow.

The hummingbirds buzzed; the loons, they hooted.

Max cocked his head and down the trail he scooted.

There was mist on the lake … an early bird's prize …

a lingering fog as the sun began to rise.

While shapes in the distance stayed blurry, not clear,

Odie drew pictures; glad none came too near!

He imagined some pirates and their rowdy crews.

Max knew they were just fishermen and a goose or two,

tipping their hats with a hearty "hello"

or honking together as they looked to and fro.

"A good morning to you!" Max waved and he flapped.

Odie was ready with his paddle and pack.

As he launched the canoe with his buddy and mate,

Odie thought, "My skipper's the best on the lake!"

Ready to steer, Odie took to the stern.

Max posed in the bow with his paws planted firm.

"He's silly and so cute!" Odie held in his giggles.

Max sat very still. Boats are no place for wiggles.

With a reach and a pull, they paddled their way

to a spot on the lake where there were loons at play;

not a pair and their chick swimming in a row,

but six in a circle ... hooting high and low.

Such a curious sight Odie had never seen,

and Max's interest was certainly keen.

The loons swam and danced and dove for their grub.

Max woofed and he wagged at this odd breakfast club.

"Shh! Max, let's give them their space,

or they'll dive and come up in a whole new place!"

With a hush in his paddle, Odie eased away,

then reached for his notes and knew just what to say.

Before he could jot even one thing or two,

Max looked to the left and his tail swooshed a clue

that two crusty old turtles were plopped on a rock,

sunning themselves on their own private dock!

Max barked a cheerful "Hey, you! Want to play?"

With a nod in their necks, they both seemed to say,

"Just hangin' here is the way life should be.

Lake life's in the slow lane! Don't you agree?"

Odie paused to consider the turtle's wise words.

Max climbed up and got cozy. He, too, had heard.

The once frisky pup became settled and still.

With his belly on the seat, Max knew how to chill!

Together, they paddled past all kinds of sights,

feeling happy to have neighbors who are such a delight—

like a moose in a cove munching grasses and weeds ...

like dragonflies so vivid they seem to wear beads …

like a blue heron standing majestic and tall ...

or the lily pad carpet whose white blossoms sprawl!

Filled with the visions of a super-swell cruise,

Odie thought to himself, "My pooch is my muse!

We're a big, happy family here at the lake.

I'm so glad my buddy, Max, nudged me awake."

Meet the Neighbors

Mr. Moose

- Weighs up to 1000 pounds and may be 7 feet tall at the shoulders (WHOA!)
- Can be seen most often at dawn or dusk
- Is saying "back away" if the hairs on his hump are raised, his ears are laid back, or he's licking his lips
- Sometimes runs up to 35 mph
- May stay underwater for 30 seconds while he swims

Madam Heron

- Only weighs 5 or 6 pounds (MUST BE THOSE HOLLOW BONES!)
- Flies almost as fast as Mr. Moose runs
- Has a wing span of $5\frac{1}{2}$ - 6 feet
- Wades and waits; then strikes like lightning
- Hunts by day and night (WOW! NIGHT VISION!)

Lady Lily Pad

- Frogs hang out on her leaves
- In summer, her "shade" keeps fish cool
- Green on top and purple on the bottom (COOL COLORS!)
- Blossoms and hollow stems send air to her roots
- American Indians used her leaves for healing

Odie's Fun Facts

Sir Turtle

- Can stay underwater for 3 hours
- Hibernates by digging into mud and leaves
- Can live 40 years (NOW THAT'S CRUSTY!)
- He's sneaky! A wriggly-wormy growth on the end of his tongue helps him capture fish. When fish come toward the "worm," he SNAPS them into his jaws!
- If you see him on land, leave him alone!

Mr. & Mrs. Loon

- Tremolo, wail, yodel and hoot: the 4 coolest calls ever heard on a lake (I WONDER WHAT EACH ONE MEANS!)
- So graceful on water; so clumsy on land
- Usually hang out by themselves, but once there were 6 on the lake (WEIRD and FUN!)
- Nesting platforms help Mom and Dad protect their eggs and chicks. (GIVE THEM THEIR SPACE!)

Dame Dragonfly

- She eats on the "fly;" looks like a helicopter darting up and down
- Dragonfly dinner specials: fried mosquitoes (HA!)
- Has been around for 30 million years
- Big, buggy eyes give her amazing vision

**Learn more and have fun with *Once Around the Lake* activities.
Visit: www.susanwoodsgolder.com**

Dr. Susan Woods Golder, Author

Susan has always loved writing. The beauty, the magic, and the power of words inspire her. She is a former teacher, writing coach, and Director of Elementary and Secondary Education and Professional Development. Over the course of her career, Susan has trained hundreds of teachers and facilitated workshops throughout the country on both effective instructional practices and curricular programs. As founder of Woodsgolder Associates, Susan provides educational and organizational consulting to school leaders as they strive to meet the learning needs of their students.

Susan holds a master's and doctoral degree in Educational Leadership and Instructional Design. She is a member of the Society of Children's Book Writers and Illustrators. Susan and her husband, Charlie (and Max) live in the western lakes and mountains region of Maine where the tall pines, blue skies and still waters give them a "wow" every day.

Visit Susan at: www.susanwoodsgolder.com

Daniel Traynor, Illustrator

Misty mornings and colorful sunsets were a big part of Daniel Traynor's childhood. Having grown up on a lake, Daniel's creativity was sparked by the ***Once Around the Lake*** project. He has been drawing for as long as he can remember. As a child, Daniel spent his first allowance on a children's book so he could study the illustrations and begin to develop his unique artistic style. He holds a Bachelor of Fine Arts degree and has worked in the art field for his entire career—first as a graphic artist, and now as an illustrator and caricaturist.

Visit Dan at: danieltraynor66@yahoo.com

Made in the USA
Middletown, DE
14 July 2015